D1452871

WIZARDS IN SPACE SAMPLER

VOLUME 1

FICTION VORTEX™

Fictionite™

Join the Story with
our groundbreaking mobile app
http://www.fictionite.io
Redefining digital narrative.

TABLE OF CONTENTS

Wizards in Space StoryVerse™ Sampler
Eugene Morgulis, Vivian Belenky, Camille Kietzman, Leenna Naidoo

ISBN: 978-1-947655-05-8
Published by Fiction Vortex, Inc. (FV Press)
Nampa, ID 83651
http://www.fictionvortex.com

Wizards in Space Cover by Vivian Belenky
Voyages of the Ivory Scepter Cover by Daniel Priego
Quest for the Wholly Pale Cover by László Zakariás of tsg pictures
Chaos Theory Cover by Vivian Belenky
My Fair Dragon Cover by Vivian Belenky

Published in the United States of America

NOTE TO THE READER

WELCOME TO *WIZARDS IN SPACE*, a StoryVerse™ of the Fiction Vortex™ (www.fictionvortex.com). You may have gathered that this project involves a growing handful of uncouth authors bent on creating a ruckus amongst the publishing establishment. Shame on us. But kudos to you for boldly stepping into the Vortex.

Wizards in Space is a StoryVerse™. That means many different authors are creating many different series within a shared story-world. Fiction Vortex publishes these series via weekly (or even daily) episodes. An episode will typically range anywhere from 30 to 60 pages.

You may choose to follow any or all of the series within a StoryVerse. Each series is designed to be enjoyable independently of the others. Of course the series will enhance each other and shed light on the story world as a whole.

Current *Wizards in Space* Series: (as of October 2017)

- Voyages of the Ivory Scepter by Eugene Morgulis
- Quest for the Wholly Pale by Leenna Naidoo
- Chaos Theory by Vivian Belenky
- My Fair Dragon by Camille Kietzman

No one knows exactly how long each StoryVerse will remain open (actively publishing regular content). But we promise that once we start a StoryVerse, we'll end it eventually. No leaving everyone hanging like a certain Fox Studio.

I suspect that *Wizards in Space* will easily require a couple years worth of continual episodes to draw to its climactic closure. But if it balloons in popularity and scope, who knows where it will go before it's all over. This is, after all, a live process depending in no small part on your participation.

So head on over to our website or download our mobile app, Fictionite, and sign up for a free account if you wish to get more involved.

For now, enjoy *Wizards in Space*. And remember…

It's Wizards… In Space!

WIZARDS IN SPACE SAMPLER

VOLUME 1

A Fiction Vortex Series

HIS GREATEST ILLUSION WAS BEING A HERO

Voyages OF THE IVORY SCEPTER

EUGENE MORGULIS

VOYAGES OF THE
IVORY SCEPTER

EUGENE MORGULIS

Episode 1: Bildenploy's Gambit

One

ARCHMAGE FOSTER BILDENPLOY STROKED his beard as he studied the image of the hulking dungeon ship on the main crystal ball. It was a Guild-commissioned astral vessel, like his own *Ivory Scepter*, so there wasn't any obvious cause for concern. But Foster was too shrewd and too cautious to ignore the uneasy feeling in the pit of his stomach.

"Wards up," he said.

Chief Security Mage Glindon Shafley nodded and whispered an incantation into his thaumaturgic transceiver. "Wards in place, Archmage," he said with his left mouth, as his right mouth finished the shielding spell.

"Ms. Plink," said Foster. "Any abnormal intuitions about that vessel?"

The fairy tapped her ear points with two tiny fingers and furrowed her brow in deep concentration. "Uncertain, Archmage. The aura readings on board the *Golem* are normal. Crew and prisoners are all accounted for, but..." Bix Plink bit her lip and flew to the crystal ball, pressing her hands against its smooth milky surface.

"Strange," she said under her breath. "My intuition readings keep shifting randomly. It's like I'm getting some kind of stochastic feedback."

Foster's eyes went wide. "Bix! Get away from there!"

But it was too late. Bix's delicate body twisted violently, and her glow shifted from yellow to red to purple. In an instant, she was sucked into the orb, her high-pitched scream fading with her.

"I need a probability stabilization field around the entire ship!" shouted Foster. "Anything you've got against chaos magic."

Glindon looked at him incredulously. Chaos magic was dangerous and unpredictable, which is precisely why the Guild outlawed it ages ago. But Foster Bildenploy expected his crew to be ready for anything.

"Just do it, Glin!"

Glindon swung back to his console and began whispering rapidly out of both mouths. Foster listened closely, offering corrections and variations. They just managed to sever the connection that had ensnared Bix when a dark cackle interrupted their enchantments.

"Not fast enough, Foster," said a creaky voice. "Not fast enough."

The mages on the bridge turned to the crystal ball, where the prison ship had been replaced by a horrible face. Two blue eyes blazed inside a storm cloud of black and white hair, from which a long, thin nose shot accusingly. It was a face Foster had not seen for over two decades.

"Kroven!" spat Foster, pounding his armrest. "But how?"

"How did I escape?" said the old warlock with a bemused, pedantic air. "Tell me, Foster, do you know what even a small chaos bubble can do when introduced into the brain of a dim-witted prison guard? Especially one with horns on his head that act like thaumaturgical antennae? No? Well, he becomes highly suggestible and most accommodating to a prisoner's demands. Before his mind shatters, that is." Kroven chuckled. "Wonderful stuff, chaos magic. It comes at a price, of course."

Kroven raised his left hand to reveal that three of his fingers were missing. The cost of chaos. "But don't worry, Foster. I've got something to help me with that."

The mages gasped when they saw what Kroven held in his other hand.

Even with her glow dimmed and her wings crumpled, the fairy retained the delicate grace that immediately caught Foster's attention when she first floated onto the *Ivory Scepter* as part of the Guild's Fairy Inclusion pilot program. She was stronger than she looked, much stronger. But Kroven's magic was stronger still.

"Bix! No!" gasped Foster.

"Did I detect a hint of sentiment for this creature?" said Kroven, smacking his lips. "Tisk Tisk, Foster. You should really be more careful with your loyal crewmages."

"Let her go!" Foster demanded.

Kroven mulled over the demand for several moments as he rolled Bix's tiny body in his palm. "No," he said finally, and crunched down on her skull like a carrot.

Glindon screamed out of one mouth and said a prayer with the other. Aldorra Grunn, the *Ivory Scepter's* chief healer, muffled a sob with her hands. After a moment, the bridge fell silent, but for the faint hum of its illumination orbs and the bubbling of various navigational potions.

On the crystal ball's display, Kroven grinned wide and waggled the fingers that had reappeared on his left hand, good as new, demonstrating fairy blood's restorative effect on post-chaos appendage displacement. Being harvested for their blood was the stuff of fairy nightmares.

Foster allowed a single sigh before he forced himself to put Bix out of his mind. He regarded the newly whole warlock with a steely, calculating gaze. "What do you want, you monster?"

"Only what I am owed, Foster! I want to be instated as Archmage Supreme. I want my own astral ship—Griffon class or higher. I want my contributions to the field of interstellar sorcery recognized by the Academy. I want..."

As Kroven listed various grievances and demands, Foster tucked his hands beneath his blue robes and began scribbling on his palm. As he did, words appeared in the *Ivory Scepter's* barracks:

SECURITY TEAM TO TRANSPORTAL ROOM. WANDS ON STUN.

Foster glanced at the display to make sure that Kroven was still droning on.

"And most of all, so-called 'Archmage Bildenploy,' I want you to suffer. I want you to know the pain of losing your position, your life's work, your..."

A tiny vibration from his signet ring told Foster that the security team had jumped through the portal. They had orders to make their way through the *Golem*, unenchanting or, if necessary, subduing her enthralled crew, and then to take down Kroven by any means.

"Foster, are you listening?" Kroven sounded annoyed.

"Yes, yes. Fourteen centaur concubines. Was that male or female?"

"Some of each. And here I thought you were distracted thinking about your strike team. You needn't bother."

Foster blinked, then hurriedly pulled out his owl feather and tapped it on his earlobe.

"Bildenploy to away team," he whispered. "What happened? Where are you?"

There was no response, so Foster tapped his ear

again and tried channeling Krom. Then Phineas. Then
Kevin. None answered.

"What have you done to them?" he growled into
the orb.

"Nothing at all," said Kroven. "I did, however,
encase this vessel in an outcome-refracting prism, so
that anyone trying to portal onto it would be deposited
in a random spot in the galaxy. A rather advanced bit of
chaos magic that cost me both feet, but your delicious
fairy girlfriend fixed that too."

"Where are my mages, you villainous barnacle?"
screamed Foster.

"Well that's the beauty of chaos, dear boy. They
could be anywhere. On some barren moon. Inside a
neutron star. Look, there's one behind you!"

Foster spun around, but saw nothing. When he
turned back, Kroven was falling out of his chair
laughing.

"You looked! I can't believe you actually looked."
Tears streamed down Kroven's hairy face. "Stars and
moons, Foster, have you actually gotten dumber since
the Academy? I don't know whose wand you polished
to get your own ship, but they must be regretting it
now. Not as much as your former crewmages, of
course, most of whom are probably suffocating in the

vacuum of space. Does the knowledge that you've sent so many Red Robes to their deaths bother you? Or are you used to it by now?"

Foster swatted over the crystal ball, and Kroven's devilish face disappeared. The warlock was only half wrong. It was not that Foster was used to death, although, in his time as Archmage of the *Ivory Scepter*, he'd certainly seen his share. Rather, it was that Foster had, long ago, forgiven himself for the lives that would be lost under his command. Greatness had a price, though it was often paid by others. Any Archmage who failed to accept this was a fool.

Two

FOSTER, ALDORRA, AND GLINDON solemnly made their way to the situational tabernacle, where they gathered with the other officers to weigh their options at the Stone Altar of Strategy.

Engaging Kroven's ship had been dismissed immediately. The *Golem* had the armor and weapons of a hydra-class warship, and while the phoenix-class *Ivory Scepter* was no sitting goose, she had been designed for exploration beyond the limits of astral projection, not major battle. Besides, as Foster was quick to remind them, there were still Guild personnel on board. To complicate the situation, Kroven was somehow jamming the *Ivory Scepter's* sub-ether communications, thus blocking any distress calls. They were on their own.

"I know it's not the most noble option," ventured Ignatius Dee, the ship's chief alchemist, "but we could make a run for it."

Foster looked at the portly alchemist and

wondered how such a yellow-bellied barnacle made it onto his crew. "A possible option," he said diplomatically. "What do the tactical divinations tell us?"

All eyes fell upon Helga Moxley-Pox, as the wizened crone slammed a dusty tome upon the altar. After a scabrous lick of her thumb, she flipped through the pages, grunting when she had found the right charts. The others waited in silence as the witch fumbled in her robes, finally producing a bag from which she pulled several small lizards, slit open their bellies with a jagged fingernail, and spat in the wounds. She then smeared their entrails in two lines across the stone.

"The *Golem's* too fast," she whispered after studying the gore pattern. "She'd overtake us before we reached the nearest Guild outpost."

Foster cursed. The other mages sat in silence.

"We need to get Kroven off that ship," he said finally, rubbing his temples. "And the only way to do that, is to offer him something he wants."

"But you heard his list of demands," said Aldorra. "They're—"

"Insane!" interjected Glindon with his unruly left mouth. Such an outburst would have gotten him reprimanded on any other ship, but Foster let it go. He valued his chief security mage's loyalty as much as his spellcasting.

Foster drummed his fingers on the altar. "Kroven was just toying with us," he said after some thought. "What he really wants is me."

The assembled mages began to chatter, but Foster silenced them with a raise of his hand. He then sighed and proceeded to recount how, years ago, Kroven had been his mentor at the Academy. He told them of Kroven's secret laboratory beneath the witch-hazel grove where the old warlock tried to bring young Foster into his illicit study of chaos magic. Foster had been intrigued at first—that part he left out—but eventually reported Kroven to the Guild leadership, just as any young mage with half a brain would have. The scandal sent Kroven to prison, and put Foster on the path to the command he'd always dreamed of.

"That was twenty years ago," said Foster, looking around the stunned faces of his crew. "Now, Kroven is finally seeking his revenge. So I'm betting he'll be eager to face me, mage to mage."

"Archmage, that's suicide," Aldorra said softly.

Glindon nodded anxiously. "I have to agree," he said. "Kroven could use his chaos magic to, well I don't know, anything! Destabilize a whole planet maybe. Turn it inside out or into a ball of lava."

"Potentially," said Foster, rising from his seat. "Depending on how much of himself he's willing to lose. But I don't think he'll do that, at least not right away. He'll play with me for a while. Maybe he'll get cocky and give me an opening. In the meantime, you all work on getting through to the *Golem* and rescuing her crew. But be careful. Understood?"

The mages nodded.

"Merlin preserve you," said Glindon with both mouths.

THREE

PLANETOID KD-78 WAS as nondescript as one would expect of a lifeless hunk of rock with no name. It had an atmosphere of sorts, owing to a small ocean on its western hemisphere. But, from where Foster was standing, all he could see was a cracked yellow wasteland.

He was wearing every ring, charm, and amulet his crew could spare. Glindon had spent an hour putting every ward he could think of on him, as Aldorra filled his pockets with healing potions and elixirs. Foster had refused Ignatius's offer of some serious-looking incendiary crystals, guessing that they could be more liability than asset. Armed as he was, he still felt a rush of fear when the portal opened, and Kroven stepped onto the dusty ground.

"I've waited years for this," said Kroven.

"Then wait no longer," said Foster and hurled a massive fireball with all his might. The spell screamed toward Kroven, scorching the earth beneath it. He batted it aside and stabbed two fingers at Foster in riposte.

Nothing happened, but for a tiny pop.

"Brilliant, my boy," said Kroven. "You remembered my affinity for lightning attacks, so you chose a planet with a negative ion atmosphere. Very clever. But it won't save you!"

Kroven threw up his hands, and the ground beneath Foster's feet erupted. He slid down the fresh crag, and landed hard on the ground, rolling away moments before the structure crashed down on top of him. Foster barely had time to drink a bone-setting elixir and massage his ankle back into place before the rock he was using for cover exploded.

"I taught you better than that!" called Kroven.

Foster snapped his fingers and a blinding light shot out. He heard Kroven groan and rolled out from cover, launching a salvo of energy spikes from his fingertips. They zipped through the air, converging on Kroven, but puffed out like fireworks before they could damage him. Foster followed up with a pair of fireballs. Kroven deflected one and dodged the other, but he slipped on the ice Foster had blasted beneath his feet.

Foster started to feel confident and prepared another attack when he felt the ether change. He realized too late what Kroven was about to do. What came to his lips was not a spell, but a prayer.

"Protect me," he uttered, as the wave of chaos swept over him.

Several ward layers flaked off like confetti, and the others were struggling to hold their structure. But hold they did.

When Foster looked up, he saw that the chaos wave had cost Kroven a hand. But it hadn't slowed him down. Before Foster could counter, Kroven sent a focused beam of noxious randomness at him. Foster knew he couldn't take another hit head on, so he threw himself to the side. Kroven's blast winged him.

Foster screamed in pain. His side bubbled with stochastic disruption, as the living cells shifted wildly from state to state, giving off puffs of chlorine, ammonia, and cinnamon. Foster fumbled through his pockets, discarding vial after vial until he found Aldorra's anti-entropic salve, which managed to negate the roiling rash, leaving the flesh scarred but intact. He'd forgotten how much chaos stung.

"How long do you think you can hold out, Foster?" shouted Kroven, who was now missing his entire left arm.

"Longer than you by the look of it," replied

Foster with false confidence.

Kroven was not fooled. "You should have joined me. Or at least kept your mouth shut. Now I'll tear you apart piece by piece."

Kroven growled as he gathered up entropic forces around him, causing the air to crackle with improbability. Foster lobbed a few magical attacks, but they each fizzled in the swirl of chaos surrounding the warlock. With a deep bellow, Kroven raised his remaining fist to the sky and called down a torrent of disordered reality.

Foster managed to cast a few additional wards, but they only held for a moment. The stronger ones Glindon had set were collapsing quickly as well. Foster yanked an emerald ring from his finger with his teeth and swallowed it with a prodigious gulp. The added burst of power sent his heart racing, and he did his best to shore up the remaining barriers.

All around him, corporeality was boiling. Particles split and bonded at random, creating a billowing lightshow as windows to other places, times, and dimensions opened for fractions of moments and then disappeared into the boundless chasm of possibility.

Foster's strength was failing. He drank a

fortifying potion and poured another over his head, but Kroven's power overwhelmed him. Wards collapsed. Chaos encroached. And with a flash of light, it was over.

Four

WHEN FOSTER OPENED HIS eyes, he saw that he stood among a mass of undifferentiated matter. To his shock and delight, he was whole. Some of the chaos energy had made it through his shields, but thankfully, it had been absorbed by a very rare and powerful thermodynamic amulet produced from the recesses of Mrs. Moxley-Pox's bottomless robe. The concentrated uncertainty had turned the amulet's jewel into a burnt turnip.

Wearily, Foster walked over to a patch of solid-looking ground, careful to avoid hanging bits of plasma. The sky, once green, was now lilac, and the air smelled of copper. He felt lucky to be alive.

Kroven had not fared as well. Indeed, the chaos blast cost him most of his body, and he was now no more than a head and torso, hovering uneasily in the air. Even his nose was gone. And yet, when Foster approached him, he saw that Kroven's eyes were as calm as two glacial lakes.

"It appears you are out of protective trinkets," said Kroven.

Foster laughed. "It appears you are out of limbs."

"You continue to underestimate me, Foster. I'll be whole in a moment. But you'll still be defenseless."

Kroven craned his neck and tongued something from a hidden pocket over his right shoulder. Foster squinted and saw that it was a tiny leg—Bix's tiny leg. It disappeared into Kroven's mouth, which twisted unpleasantly as he swallowed what remained of the fairy. He started to laugh.

Exhausted, Foster sat on the ground and removed his boots.

"Giving up already?" called Kroven. "Not going to even attempt a last stand? I don't blame you. As soon as I...I..." Kroven clammed up when he realized that he wasn't regenerating.

"Do you know what I hate most about chaos magic?" said Foster, rubbing the empty space where his left pinky toe should have been. "It itches like hell."

"Why—why isn't anything happening?" Kroven's eyes darted in panic.

"Because I changed it," said Foster. "I transformed the fairy leg before you could swallow it." He paused to give Kroven a chance to process.

Finally, the warlock understood. "You used chaos magic," he whispered.

"Of course," said Foster. "I've been using chaos magic for years. Ever since you showed me. I had to be discreet, at first, but it got easier once Bix started providing me with doses of her fairy blood for regeneration. You would have liked her, Kroven. Ambitious. Loyal. Not afraid to get her little hands dirty, unlike those other beef-witted mealworms. You weren't supposed to eat her, you imbecile. Now I'll have to find another one. Oh well. Plenty more fairies at the Academy since the Guild granted them equal rights."

"You *planned* this?" stammered Kroven.

Foster smiled and shrugged. "Do you know how long it takes to rise through the ranks of the Guild? I mean, there's no one on the Council younger than ninety! So I got to thinking, if tattling on you helped me make Archmage, imagine what I'll get by defeating you single-handed. They'll make me a Council Magus for sure!"

"But I found you," said Kroven, bobbing in bewilderment as he struggled to stay aloft. "I bested your ship."

"Yes, and it took you long enough. I even had to

get that horn-faced clay-brain a guard position aboard the *Golem*. His name was Grozzjack, by the way. Most incompetent mage I ever commanded—not that I said so in my recommendation letter. I figured he'd give you an opening, and you took the bait as expected. Of course then I had to make sure I'd have you all to myself, which is why I sabotaged the *Ivory Scepter's* communications." Foster's voice suddenly shifted from sardonic to magnanimous. "I had no choice but to bravely face you alone."

Kroven fumed, but said nothing. Foster could sense scraps of magical energies collecting around his diminished frame for a last desperate attack.

"Can I just ask you one thing?" called Foster. "And then I promise I'll give you a free shot."

Kroven grimaced. "Ask."

"Out of all the random possibilities in the universe, what did Bix's leg turn into in your mouth? It didn't look terribly tasty."

Kroven narrowed his eyes. "Licorice."

"Oh," said Foster, disappointed.

"I hate licorice."

"Oh!" said Foster happily and launched a magic missile that severed Kroven's head from his torso.

FIVE

THE CREWMAGES OF THE *Ivory Scepter* cheered as
their Archmage returned and recounted his harrowing
battle, leaving out plenty. They whispered of his
bravery and speculated about his inevitable ascension
to the Council. Foster took it all in, dispensing with his
usual mask of humility. Why continue to pretend when
he was on the verge of getting everything he'd ever
wanted?

LEENNA NAIDOO

THIS YOUNG
WIZARD'S
NO FLY-BY
KNIGHT.

QUEST
FOR THE
WHOLLY PALE

 A FICTION VORTEX SERIES

QUEST FOR THE WHOLLY PALE

LEENNA NAIDOO

EPISODE 1: EMRYS MEETS AN OLD ONE

ONE

WHEN THE TEAL-EYED foundling who became known as Emrys first began living with the old wizard Lailoken on the planet Broceli294, many assumed the arrangement would end in disaster. But the cheerful boy and the old wizard proved them wrong, for a time. Emrys thrived with the eccentric wizard as father and mentor, as both shared an uncommon magical ability and a love of chivalric romance novels and crystal screen sagas.

All went well until Emrys Lailoken's fourteenth year, when a mysterious figure cloaked in gray arrived unannounced, angering Old Lailoken, who didn't appreciate uninvited guests or being hit in the stomach by a hurled memory crystal. With many gestures in Emrys' direction, the

two wizards exchanged hot and angry words in Old Gaelic —
an ancient wizardly tongue known only to the most
accomplished and powerful of magic-users. Before long,
wands appeared and violent magics began to fly. With a heart
full of love and courage, young Emrys rushed to his mentor's
aid, and was immediately knocked senseless.

When Emrys awoke, he found the Gray Wizard gone
and Old Lailoken despondent. With trembling lips, the broken
wizard told his ward how the mysterious stranger had cursed
the lad in a most diabolical way. And so it was that Emrys
never heard the words that cursed him to find the Wholly Pale
or suffer an early death thrice over, and to never know True
Love.

Though Old Lailoken made many attempts to remove
the curse, his magic proved as powerless against it as it had
been against the mysterious stranger. The most obvious cure,
questing to find the Wholly Pale, Old Lailoken deemed far too
dangerous and forbade Emrys from even thinking of it. Still,
as the months dragged by, Old Lailoken grew increasingly
distraught over his failure to protect Emrys and inability to
lift the curse. During one of Old Lailoken's attempts, a
strange living Parchment was created from the boy's
suffering and bonded to young Emrys immediately. Many
believe that hidden in the strange animated text lie the clues
to finding the Wholly Pale, and perhaps the true destiny of

the boy.

Despite Old Lailoken's efforts, Emrys grew more and more withdrawn, even rebellious, as the curse settled into him.

A year to the day of the Gray Wizard's visit, Old Lailoken disappeared.

Orphaned once again and heir to all of Old Lailoken's possessions, the young wizard Emrys spent most of his time torn between searching for his foster father and seeking out the Wholly Pale. Exhausting all possibilities of finding Old Lailoken on Broceli294, Emrys took the next spaceship to the neighboring star-system. And so began his cursed quest for the Wholly Pale—a thing few know of, and fewer still know how to find.

Five years have passed since the teal-eyed wizard began his fruitless search. Each day, Emrys' heart sinks ever deeper, while the promise of an early death thrice over without knowing True Love draws ever closer.

TWO

OLAF THE HUNGRY, PURSER and gourmand, looked Emrys up and down. His green eyes narrowed at the young wizard's rangy build and soft-looking hands, grew wider at the official-looking mage badge and silver-thread lining of the dark blue cloak, then turned thoughtful at the barely concealed sword upon which Emrys drummed two long fingers.

"Recommended by Terence, were you, milord?" Olaf flipped open the ship's passenger manifest and ran a finger down the list. "A wizard of your means should be quite comfortable on the quarterdeck. Brilliant views of the stars and most of the moons we'll be passing."

"Views are not a priority. Quiet is."

Olaf's eyebrows rose. "This is *The Queen Magnificent*, milord! Quiet and relaxation is all you'll find on board, along with the best meals in all known galaxies. Not to mention..." Olaf cleared his throat, heeding Emrys' furrowed brow and teal-eyed glare. He snapped shut the manifest. "Your luggage, milord?"

"I travel light."

Olaf gestured with grace. "This way, milord. The Stone Room is both soundproof and warded to the highest standards. You are guaranteed peace and quiet, or my name's not Olaf."

"Thank you."

Olaf turned right into a long sumptuously decorated corridor. "Might I be so bold as to inquire the reason for your travel?"

Emrys hesitated, but he saw no reason not to share. He'd often learned of interesting facts in this way. "I'm seeking the Wholly Pale."

Ornate doors remained discreetly closed as the surprised purser stopped momentarily. "The Holey Pail? I imagine it would be good for watering a garden?"

"The *Wholly Pale*, not Holey Pail. And, I don't know," Emrys shrugged. "You may be right."

Olaf stopped at the end of the corridor, produced a large crystal, and slotted it into a receptacle. A wooden door inscribed with protective runes whispered, 'Open,' then did.

Olaf led the way into the luxurious stateroom and handed the crystal key to Emrys with a flourish. "Here you go, Milord Lailoken. If there is anything—"

"I'll be sure to hunt you down and ask."

Olaf's smile froze for a second before he bowed and exited.

Emrys allowed himself a small grin. Sometimes it paid to be a little intimidating. Terence the tarot-reader he might trust; of his cousin Olaf, he was not so sure. The room was more than he needed and the amenities were impressive. Through the porthole, he looked down at the last minute preparations in the launch area. Emrys took off his sword and cloak, draping the one carefully over the other on a divan. His boots slipped off next as he flopped onto the floating bed with a sigh.

After a few moments of blissful relaxation, he drew out his old battered Parchment and held it above him. The animated document was held together by strong magic. Its silver runes jumbled for attention, or ran away from the eye in alarm. Emrys, in a fit of frustration, crumpled Parchment and hurled it at the porthole. It hit the glass, fell to the floor, uncrumpled itself, and began inching back to him. This was the living embodiment of his curse—written cryptic messages continuously reminding him of his misfortune in being made to seek the Wholly Pale or else suffer no love, madness, and an early death three times over.

A muffled voice interrupted his thoughts. "Well, Doofus? Do you really think this is the best way to go about your quest? Seems somewhat expensive."

Though Emrys was a loner, he was seldom completely alone. Emrys looked towards his draped cloak where Dierder resided in his portal pocket. Without moving from the comfy bed Emrys said, "Don't call me Doofus. The tarot was explicit. I have to be on this ship to find out something vital. I've taken smaller chances before."

For a few moments Dierder was silent. Emrys imagined he was pulling a draught of beer.

Dierder's next words were tentative. "You know, and don't take this the wrong way, but I'm thinking that maybe not everything wrong in your life is due to that curse."

Emrys jerked into a sitting position, outraged, causing Parchment to pause in its journey back to him. "What do you mean?"

"I mean—"

"The Gray Wizard almost killed Old Lailoken and he cursed me!"

"Yes, but about that curse—"

"An early death thrice over, no True Love, madness if I don't find the wretched thing! How, *how*, could this not be the root cause of my troubles? To search the galaxies for the Wholly Pale—"

"A thing few know of, and fewer still know how to find," droned Dierder like an old memory crystal, then paused, presumably to sip his beer.

Emrys flopped back onto the bed. Parchment took the opportunity to creep over and fold itself into his trews pocket. He stared out the porthole at the vast blackness he would once again travel, his heart cold and heavy.

Dierder sighed. "Might be simpler if you just went mad again."

Emrys was silent a long time. He had briefly tried being mad but had found it too tiresome and boring. It was a terrible curse to be insane, but more so to have to seek the Wholly Pale. He said, "I have a small hope; one day I'll find The Wholly Pale, True Love, and live to be a good old mage. Until I lose that hope, I'll continue my search."

"But is that not also a different type of madness?"

"Dierder?"

"Yes?"

"Shut up."

A long faint slurp reached Emrys' ears and he

closed his eyes, imagining what it would be like to win a fair lady's heart and rescue her from a fate worse than death, just like in Old Lailoken's fading parchment books.

The room vibrated. The ship would launch in a few minutes, and once they reached cruising speed, dinner would be served. Emrys' stomach rumbled in anticipation. He'd missed lunch yet again, and dinner on board this luxurious ship was sure to be a feast.

"Dierder?"

From the depths of his inner cloak pocket came a faint answer.

"I'll be needing my good shirt."

THREE

THE DINING ROOM WAS spacious and discerning. Through the ship's largest viewport, the Andromedan Galaxy was visible only as a dizzying whirl of pinpricks of light. It hardly seemed the ship was hurtling across space. When the spaceship slowed down for their first planet of call, the local solar system in all its glory would be revealed. Emrys, alone at his table, ate a heavenly meal at leisure. After stuffing his second helping into his pocket for Dierder, he stood up and made for the exit.

A lovely maiden stepped onto his path. "A thousand excuses, milord, but are you Emrys Lailoken?"

Emrys cleared his throat, annoyed at his customary shyness around maidens. "Yes, I am."

Her smile was delighted. "My master, Graandas the Unicorn, wishes to speak to you."

Emrys hid his surprise well. Graandas was the oldest known unicorn and an honorary adviser to the

Archmage Council. Some said he was older than the Magiclysm and had run along the hidden valleys on Earth before its despoliation. "It would be my pleasure."

The maiden bowed and led the way. As Emrys turned into the corridor, his eyes glued to the maiden's swaying form, a soft body crashed into him.

A slim hand steadied itself on his hip as she said, "Watch where you're going, Oaf!"

Emrys stared open-mouthed at the rude maiden, who stared back at him with cool silver eyes, tilted at the corners.

"Well? What are you gawking at? It's not like you've never seen a maiden before." Her glance at Emrys' guide was dismissive.

"I, I..." Emrys cleared his throat, cursing his shyness. "I beg your pardon, milady. It won't happen again."

She looked him up, then down. "Hmm," she said, then drifted into the dining room.

Emrys shook his head and sneezed as Graandas's maiden urged him forward. His allergies were acting up again. Drinking his allergy potion, Emrys wondered if his nose was tickling only because of the presence of the unicorn, or was there a basilisk around? There were no griffins around, of that he was sure. Those always brought on a terrible rash on his arms which no allergy potion could suppress, a terrible bane from his childhood. Besides, most griffins had been conscripted by the Guild.

Four

GRAANDAS LAY ON A low floating bed, his shiny ivory hooves hanging over the sides as he chewed on a tuft of straw and smoked a pipe simultaneously. Two maidens attended his silver mane while a third played a soothing tune on a golden harp. Emrys hadn't expected the old rumor to be true, but here was proof. Unicorns were, indeed, vain sybarites. Bowing before the venerable equine, he stored that knowledge away, not sure if he would have need of it later. There were no viewports or even small portholes in this suite. The Old One did not care to be reminded they traveled across the stars, Emrys surmised. Nor did the unicorn appear to have the room's wards active; perhaps he did not care for security either.

"Ah, Emrys Lailoken. I have long wished to meet you," declared Graandas.

"It is only a pleasure, Sire."

"One would hope. One will see." The unicorn paused, then puffed out a cloud of vanilla incense.

"Before I get to that which I wish to speak of, I would very much like to see that curious artifact which has been bestowed upon you."

Emrys took a moment to decipher the request and failed. "I beg your pardon, Sire?"

"That curious parchment which the Good Wizard Lailoken bestowed upon you. I have heard tell of it from the Archmages.

"Oh, you mean Parchment?"

Graandas bowed his head regally, almost stabbing the harpist.

Emrys wondered how word had gotten out about the result of his father's attempt at lifting his curse, yet no word had come about the mysterious stranger in gray who had been the cause of it all. Could this Old One help him read Parchment? He patted his cloak pocket, then the other, a look of puzzlement crossing his face. He tried his trews pocket next, and his shirt. With conflicted emotions he said, "I'm afraid I seemed to have lost it."

"Lost it? That is impossible, Boy!"

"But it's not..." Emrys recovered. "It must have been stolen by that beautiful maiden."

Emrys' maiden guide shrieked in outrage as Graandas bellowed. "Nonsense! Utter nonsense! All my maidens are the purest of pure. One is appalled that you would even consider such a thing."

"Oh, not her! The other maiden. The one who bumped into me at the dining room entrance. The one with those tilted silver eyes—"

"A thief!" roared Graandas, never moving a lazy muscle save for his mouth, his pipe and tuft of grass fixed to his lip. "Here on this ship! Notify the captain. Notify the guards. This will not be tolerated!"

The maidens hurried hither and thither. The harpist tapped a glitter-encrusted feather, frantically trying to call the emergency line. Two other maidens opened the suite door. Outside crouched four men clad in black, striking menacing poses and brandishing crystal swords. A bored-looking ogre loomed above them, casually holding the largest crystal sword of all. They could only be unicorn slayers. Expert unicorn slayers who had come with the only known weapons capable of killing unicorns. Expert assassins who flipped and crouched into an unassailable formation— four men in a fan, ogre in the middle, sword making a point.

Graandas screamed in fear along with his maidens. Hampered by his lazy bones, it was all he could do just then. Emrys sprang into action, grateful for his wiztial arts training. Whipping out a *Minutes-Slow* potion, he threw it at the slayers, buying Graandas time. Wasting no normal instant, he shoved the unicorn onto his hooves and pulled the maidens to safety.

One look at Graandas's eyes rolling with fear told him the unicorn would be of no help in the coming fight. Emrys hung his head and sighed. He so hated saving maidens, never mind a venerable unicorn. They were always so embarrassingly grateful afterwards. How to accept thanks and speak to maidens had never been on his schooling subjects, or even brought up in those long chats with Old Lailoken who seemed perfectly fine in the company of those dowagers and genteel witches who frequented their forest home. So much to learn, so few books...and Broceli294 maidens.

Graandas and his maidens screamed again.

Emrys straightened up, tall and true, frantically sifting through his repertoire of spells to counter crystal swords and ogres. Then he smiled, his teal eyes glowing with glee. He so seldom got to do what he was about to do. "Dierder, my Number Two, please," he whispered.

A metal wand with two small silk-covered protrusions slipped from his pocket and into his waiting hand. His finger slid along, setting it to Lethal.

Five

THE OGRE LED THE charge, just as Emrys had hoped. A flick of his wrist sent a violent vibration of sound down the Number Two and out the reverberating silk protrusions towards the fearsome fiends.

The ogre screamed. The terrifying chord whipping their brain into numbness. Their four companions dodged their toppling body and faced the teal-eyed wizard who stood grinning back at them.

"We just want the Old One," hissed the bravest of the slayers.

"Drop your swords," replied Emrys, his voice clear and steady.

A whinny of fear from Graandas broke the tense silence. The bravest slayer bellowed a war-cry, leading the others in a rush at the wizard.

Emrys whirled his wand in a high arc, producing a piercing tone which hurt the ears of everyone and cracked the crystal swords. The slayers paused.

"Drop. Your. Swords. The crystal will shatter,

whatever you do with them."

"Crystal shards can kill unicorns as well, you silly boy!" whinnied Graandas.

"What he said," said the bravest slayer.

"I know. People too," was Emrys' unfazed reply. "So let me make things *crystal* clear."

The weakest slayer took a step back as Emrys whipped up the wand and swirled it around, stirring up a high whine. With his other hand, he cast shields of silence and protection, then threw them over himself, the unicorn, and the maidens. With the rising pitch came the men's screams of agony. Two dropped their swords, holding their bloodied ears, and ran off. The remaining two and the ogre died by their own swords, the flying shards devastating every living thing (and then some) without a shield in the suite.

Emrys dropped the shields as the last fragments of crystal tinkled onto the floor.

Into the shocked natural silence, Graandas said, "I have never seen the like. That wand is most wondrous."

Emrys turned the metal wand around in his hand. "Crafted by the great smith, Gibson himself."

Six

"I MUST NOW SPEAK of the thing which I wished to speak of before we were so rudely interrupted," said Graandas, restored once more to his floating bed and smoking a pipe while chewing a tuft of new grass.

"I..." Emrys twitched involuntarily. The grateful maiden who was massaging his neck and shoulders had also tickled his ears. "...am intrigued."

"So you should be. One has much to share, and One wishes to enlighten you."

Like the tilted silver-eyed maiden, thought Emrys, but said nothing. He had learned never to look a gift horse in the mouth and wasn't about to start now.

Graandas cleared his throat dramatically. "One knows of what you must seek should you wish to be rid of the...curse, as you call it."

Emrys stood up abruptly, having turned an unbecoming shade of red. He could no longer endure the attention of the grateful massaging maiden. Immediately, his former guide presented him with a glass of Amethyst Ichor mined by little-known denizens on the hidden planetoid Alpha C78. He waved the glass away oblivious to the girl's crestfallen look. "Please, go on, Sire. Any help in my quest would be uncommonly appreciated."

Graandas shook his regal head, throwing the third maiden, who was attending his mane, into the harpist. "It is the least I can do, especially with you saving my horn as efficiently as you did. It has been a long time since I have faced slayers, much less such well-equipped and informed ones. That ogre would have been the death of me had the other four men failed."

Emrys made no reply, but began pacing as the unicorn spoke.

Graandas continued. "That which holds the vital key to removing the...curse from you, is One's most ancient of enemies—"

"The Order of Chaos?"

Graandas stared fixedly at Emrys, who realized his error. Graandas didn't take kindly to such arcane knowledge from one as young as he. Old Lailoken had warned him about such Old Ones.

Emrys, trying to cover up his gaffe, said quickly, "The Merchants of Sirius B12?"

Graandas's glare would have frozen lesser mortals and a few immortals. "One is imparting vital little-known, even *secret*, information. One does not like to be interrupted at such times."

Emrys looked contrite and made apologies, remembering his policy on gift horses. Avoiding the eye of the simpering harpist, he implored, "Please, Sire. Go on."

Mollified, the ancient unicorn puffed out sandalwood incense and continued. "You must seek out the resting place of the Great Merlin. There you shall find the means of eradicating this...curse that plagues you. You might even find the Wholly Pale, though I doubt it."

Emrys took an eager step forward. "You've heard of the Wholly Pale?"

Graandas snickered. "Heard of it? How could One not?"

Emrys knelt at the unicorn's hooves. "What is it? What does it do? Where do I find it?"

Graandas would not meet the anxious young wizard's eye, closing his own instead as he inhaled deeply on sandalwood smoke. "One cannot help you further. Seek the resting place of the Great Merlin. That is all One can say."

Disappointed, Emrys sighed and hung his head, sensing his quest had just gotten more complicated.

"One may add that One is certain you shall find what you are *truly* seeking. If that is the Wholly Pale and the whole of it, One has ascertained that you shall unearth it."

It wasn't much use, but Emrys felt grateful the unicorn now had such faith in him. He seldom had such in himself these five long years since Old Lailoken disappeared.

SEVEN

EMRYS AWOKE IN HIS suite to a stealthy rustling. Parchment was back. It crept unhurriedly under the covers into his shirt pocket and settled in its customary way. Emrys felt the weight of his curse crash down on him once more. Turning his head in sadness, he stared out the porthole. A large ringed planet with three moons drifted slowly by, even as two planetoids wheeled into view. *The Queen Magnificent* was drifting towards its first planet of call, the planetoid Bluto.

A furtive sound near the door drew Emrys' attention, though he did not turn his head. Someone was in his room. He shifted under the covers and spotted the intruder almost immediately. For a second he wondered why she hadn't worn an invisibility cloak, only to remember that any spells, save his own, would not work in his room. Was she after Parchment again?

Feigning sleep, through lowered eyelids he watched the silver-eyed thief pick up his cloak and run questing fingers along it. Almost immediately,

Dierder's square, six-fingered hand emerged from the cloak pocket and swatted at her. Startled, she jumped back, holding a hand to her mouth. Silently thanking his pocket-portal companion, Emrys giggled. She whirled to face him. Their eyes met again. For a long moment, both stared transfixed. The room shuddered as *The Queen Magnificent* slowed towards its Bluto berth. Then she was leaping away, seeking her exit.

Emrys tossed off the covers and dived for her. He missed, grabbing empty air. She had the suite door open before he could regain his feet. He threw a holding spell at her, but she was already over the threshold and her own wards countered. Emrys launched himself forward, but he was too late. He stumbled through the door just in time to see the lady a few feet down the corridor. She turned, giving him a bewitching smile as she vanished.

Emrys swore and ran a hand over his face and his hair. The lady-thief could be anywhere on Bluto by now, or even on one of the nearby moons or rooms. He could open a thousand portals and still not find her. Emrys hung his head and sighed. If only his evil afflictions didn't keep ruining his luck, he could ask her how she knew about Parchment and why was she so intent on stealing it?

Back in his suite, Emrys watched the spaceship's berth draw larger and larger, blotting out the purple curve of Bluto's sphere, which was dotted with cyan storms and green continents.

Deep in his heart Emrys knew it was just a matter of time before he met the lady-thief again. With that knowledge, the heaviness of his curse seem to lift just a little. Who knew? Maybe she would lead him to the Wholly Pale or know of Merlin's resting place.

Emrys smiled. One could dream, couldn't one?

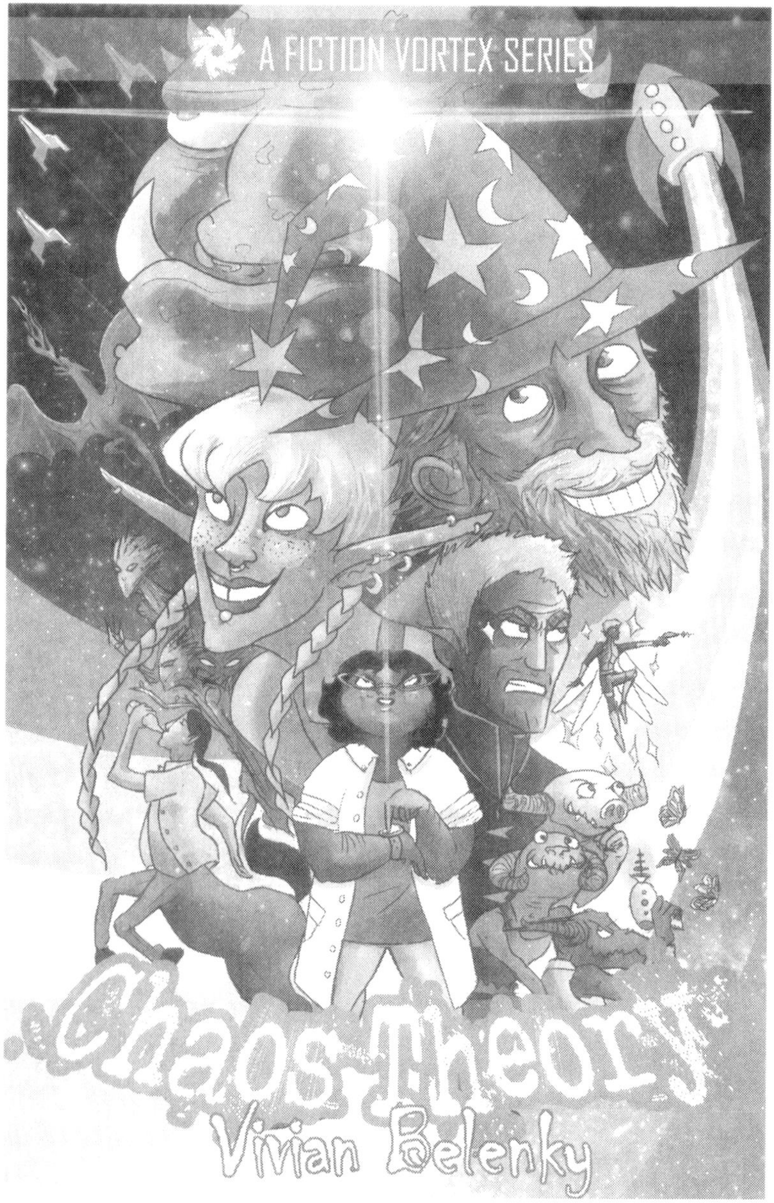
A FICTION VORTEX SERIES
Chaos Theory
Vivian Belenky

CHAOS THEORY

VIVIAN BELENKY

EPISODE 1: MURPHY'S LAW

ONE

MARGOT GUNDER WOKE ON the day of her thesis defense right as the crystal ball on her bedside table announced sixth hour. She jumped out of bed—she was obliged to jump, due to her height—and began her morning battle with the magic mirror on the wall. She considered it an omen of good luck that it took her only three tries to get it to display her reflection, rather than any number of the useless other things it habitually did, like distant mist-covered planets and beautiful princesses trapped on asteroids by wicked dragons.

Margot had no patience for princesses, beautiful or otherwise, nor for dragons, no matter how wicked. Today was the day all her efforts would come to fruition.

She brushed her teeth and hair, and shaved, lamenting the bizarre human preoccupation with female facial hair. Back on her home planet of Duluth-9, she usually didn't bother to shave her beard until it was long enough for it to get itchy—but this was hardly the most onerous thing she'd had to put up with amongst humans.

She switched the magic mirror to the news channel as she got dressed. While the news droned on about an escaped goblin criminal, she debated the professionalism of the blue robe with yellow stars versus that of the red robe with silver moons, and whether or not the glittering pointy hat was too much or just enough. She nearly skipped breakfast, before deciding that today was simply too important, and had a quick pixie dust protein shake on her way out the door. She was well-rested; bright-eyed; bushy-tailed. She was going to do *wonderfully.* She was sure of it.

Margot checked her watch, an absurdly expensive marvel of dwarven technology given to her by her mother as a passive-aggressive graduation present. It had over a thousand functions after six years of Margot's special modifications, including telling time in over three hundred different standards. Eighth bell—

she had three standard hours until her defense. She ought to speak to her advisor. Get a pep talk, maybe some last minute advice. The visiting professor's tower was nearly all the way across campus, and navigating between buildings hadn't become much easier with the years.

She blinked in the diffuse, yellow-pink morning light of Arcana, the gaseous, carbon-dioxide-rich moon which housed the Academy. Apocryphal school legend held that the Academy had once been located in one of the huge cities of Anthropus, until the magical experiments and rowdy late-night parties of the students caused the city to issue an ordinance kicking the Academy off-world. The elegant ivory buildings themselves had been lifted by the faculty with almighty levitation spells and settled in the atmosphere of Arcana, floating through the clouds, in what was surely not any kind of heavy-handed metaphor.

Margot was a scientist, and like most scientists, a dwarf. There had been a few non-dwarven students at the Institute of Gnomatics, where Margot had done her undergraduate double-degree in astrophysics and mechanical engineering, but few had excelled in the rigorous dwarven style of thinking. But Margot *had* excelled, graduating near the top of her class. Her mother, a brilliant physicist and astronaut, had been so proud. Her whole family had been thrilled, showering her with praise and gifts and advice. She was headed for a brilliant career in any forward-looking field she wanted, she was certain. Employers were practically begging at the door. She was the pride and joy of the Gunder clan. She was going to do amazing things.

And then she had decided to do a graduate degree in magical studies at the Academy, prompting the largest family argument in four generations of Gunders.

That had been six standard years ago now.

"Margot!" It was Nilia Titania, a fairy, and one of Margot's closest friends...well, only friend. She zoomed excitedly towards her, alighting on a bannister. "Watcha up to? Listen! I wanted to tell you about this totally exciting—"

"Not now, Nils," Margot said irritably. "My defense is in three hours. I was about to go talk to my advisor."

"Oh, cool! I'll fly with you!"

Margot sighed. "I don't fly, remember, Nilia?"

"Oh, right," said the fairy. She paused. "You really should, you know! It's so much faster than taking the pods."

"I realize that, Nilia," said Margot, climbing into one of the pods designated for the students who couldn't fly. The Academy had only agreed to install them after Margot had sent three angry letters and finally threatened to sue if they didn't provide her with accommodations. "I'm just not that great at magic, so I'd rather not risk it."

"Oh, yeah," said Nilia. "I keep forgetting about you dwarves and your magic problems. That's what I really don't get about you, Marge! You can't even do magic, and you're still here, plugging away with your— uh, what's it called? Sky-ence?"

"Science," Margot corrected. She wondered, not for the first time, if all fairies were like this or if that was just Nilia. "And dwarves are perfectly capable of doing magic. It's just our stupid cultural prejudice that stops us from catching up with everyone else, magically speaking." She paused, some dredge of ethnic pride welling up in her. "Although, mind you, we get along just as well as everyone else without magic. If we *did* use it, imagine how far we might have gone by now! In fact, imagine how far humans—and fairies, too—could go if they'd only apply scientific thinking to their magic! Imagine, Nilia!"

But Nilia staunchly refused to imagine it. Her

eyes had already glazed over, as nearly everyone's did whenever Margot started talking about her research. At least now, after all these years, Margot had developed a knack for noticing it.

But she was determined for that not to be the case today. She had a plan, and it would be so marvelous, so unexpected, so miraculous, that the committee would have no choice but to take her seriously.

"Anyway, the point is," said Margot, attempting to recapture Nilia's attention, "that just because we dwarves are so used to doing everything with science doesn't mean we *can't* use magic. We're just...not as used to it. Magic is a part of the world, as real as the air and the earth, so we can use science to understand it. Which is exactly what I'm doing."

"Oh," said Nilia. "My Magical Theory professor says magic comes from pixie farts and dragon wishes. Anyway, did you hear about that goblin on the news this morning? He's supposed to be a *terrible* criminal. He went on a full-scale rhyming spree last time he was loose. The whole campus is on alert, since he's on Arcana somewhere. You don't think he'll come *here*, do you? What with the protections around campus and all?"

"Your Magical Theory professor is full of crap," said Margot. "That's the problem with you magical types. Magic comes so easily to you that you never bother to think about what it really *is*."

"Yeah, uh-huh," said Nilia. She took out her powder compact and checked it for notifications. "Are you coming to the protest today?"

Margot stared blankly. "What protest?"

"Oh, you know. Students for Fairy Welfare is having a sit-in in front of the dean's office."

No recognition flickered in Margot's memory.

"About the treatment of the fairy students at this place?"

"I thought fairies already had equal rights," Margot said.

"Well, sure, but…ugh, never mind, Margot."

"But anyway, about magic," Margot went on excitedly. "I mean, just because something is difficult to understand doesn't mean it's inherently un-understandable. And sure, I haven't come up with an exhaustive scientific treatise on every aspect of magic yet—but I'm getting there!"

"Right," said Nilia, scrolling.

"After my defense today, I'll have the academic credentials to get the funding I really need to lead a full-scale research effort, and soon enough they'll be calling me all sorts of things. Unifier of Two Worlds! Mother of Magiscience!"

"Sounds cool," said the fairy. "Totally. Have fun, then."

"It's not about fun, but I will!" Margot said cheerfully as the fairy cast another levitation spell and zoomed away.

Two

FABIOCIUS GALLOWAY'S OFFICE WAS on the ground floor—insofar as a building floating in the upper atmosphere of a gaseous planet could have a "ground" floor—for which Margot was thankful, if only because stairs at the Academy were really not designed for her short legs. The door was closed, but Margot knew that he only kept it closed to avoid ever speaking to students. She rapped on the door, before becoming impatient and barging in.

"Professor Galloway?" she inquired, peeking around the door. The place was a mess. The wastebasket was overturned. Beer cans and assorted paraphernalia littered the moth-eaten rug. Horsehair covered about every available surface. Empty pizza boxes formed towers so tall they threatened to overturn. It was a bit tidier than normal, actually.

"Whozzat?" There was an abrupt snorting sound and Galloway's balding head appeared from behind the desk, followed by the rest of him. He was a centaur, the single visiting centaur professor at the Academy. Margot had assumed he had been assigned as her thesis advisor because of their mutual outsider positions.

"Hello," she said politely, bouncing a little bit on the balls of her feet. "It's me, Margot Gunder? You know, your student? I was just reminding you that my thesis defense is in," she quickly checked her watch, "two standard hours and thirty-six standard minutes, and I just wanted to make sure that you were awake and ready to sit on the defense committee and not passed out drunk under your desk."

Galloway whinnied, offended. "I'm good, I'm good," he said. "I'm up, geez." He straightened his specially tailored robes that still draped awkwardly across his horsey hindquarters. Margot noted the signature (perhaps only) tie-dyed shirt he wore under them. She really hoped he'd change soon.

"Sorry for the mess," he said, tail swishing. "I'm just, ah…a bit nervous, about a business deal. Was thinking about lying low for a while. Leaving Arcana before I…get in trouble."

"Oh," said Margot. "You mean after my defense, right?"

Galloway blinked, his tail abruptly stopped. "Right, right, yes. Of course. Your defense."

Galloway taught intergalactic law and water polo, which made him an on odd choice to assign to Margot, a pioneering scientist. Centaurs were a highly competitive people. They had invented an entire system of 'social media' so as to better judge each other, and they were the best litigators in the universe, but Margot didn't much see that in Galloway. He was the least competitive person she'd ever met. He liked to go with the flow and relax. She'd once seen him relax so hard he fell asleep in the middle of a lecture he was giving. Which still put him a notch ahead of most of his students, who usually fell asleep right at the beginning.

"So," Galloway said, "you good? Got everything in order and all that?"

"Yes!" said Margot. "Everything is fully in order sir. I just need to dash by the Great Hall a little early to set up the device for my demonstration and then I'll be ready! Just please, please, please make sure you actually show up this time and everything will be absolutely fantastic!"

"Good," said the centaur. "Great. As long as you're having fun."

Margot was already out the door. She had to make absolutely sure that the device was functioning properly before she showed it off to the committee.

THREE

MARGOT ENTERED THE GREAT Hall, tugging the device behind her on a transport cart. The Great Hall was the most beautiful room in the Academy, maybe even the whole universe. It was enchanted to display the wheeling stars and galaxies around them at an accelerated rate, so that starbirth and supernovae could be observed on a timescale of hours or even minutes. Not even a floor was visible, with only shimmering violet portals in the darkness to indicate passages to adjoining lecture halls and offices.

She paused to marvel at it all, clutching her notes and papers to her chest. This was what she was here for. The universe. Reality itself. To be described, finally, in its entirety…by her. As soon as they approved her thesis and showered her with funding.

She marveled at the beauty of the Great Hall for a moment longer, and then tugged her device into the tiny dinged-up conference room where she'd actually be giving her talk.

She spent her time carefully setting up the device. Everything had to be perfect. It wasn't even strictly necessary to have this demonstrative component, but Margot wanted to really drive home her point. So many late nights, so many missed meals, so many cups of dragonfire to have it done on time, and even so, she'd had to delay graduating by a full year now. The device was bulky, taller than Margot herself, and rather inexpertly assembled, now that she saw it with an anxious eye. Of course, she told herself, this was just the prototype. Later models would be at least tabletop-sized; she even thought that with fully integrated magitech (as she called it), she could get it small enough to serve as a portable device.

But that would be years and years from now. First things first.

Margot spent the remaining time anxiously checking her watch and soaking her robes through with sweat. There hadn't been any in her size, and she had had to hem and tailor them herself. She was suddenly painfully aware of how ridiculous it had the potential to look.

Finally it was time. The committee members began filtering into the room, though perhaps 'filtering' was the wrong word for it. Wizards, as a rule, did not filter. They pomped. They swaggered. They blustered. They swept. They hardly ever did anything as meek as filtering.

Margot anxiously counted the committee members as they pomped, swaggered, blustered, and swept inside, swirling their robes and adjusting their pointy hats as they took their seats. Margot briefly locked eyes with Ignatiolus Thrum, the head of the experimental magic department. He offered her an indulgent smile behind his beard and rolled his eyes as though to say, *very well, get on with it.*

She *would* get on with it. She would get on with it so hard that none of them would know what had hit them.

She tapped her foot nervously. Where was Galloway?

The centaur appeared seven minutes past the hour, by which time several of the committee wizards had started to get uncomfortable and distracted, absent-mindedly casting spark spells and vainly arranging their hats. As Galloway whinnied apologetically and took his seat (or, well, remained standing), a full half of the committee was no longer paying her much attention.

Well. She would just have to *demand* their

attention. That's what the demonstration was for, after all. She knew it had been a good idea.

"Greetings, Honorable Magisters," Margot began. One of the wizards yawned.

"What I am going to present today, the culmination of all my student work, is liable to change the history of magic and science forever. I'll be getting to the presentation of my thesis momentarily, but first —"

Two of the wizards audibly sighed. One even groaned softly.

"But first," Margot ground onward, "I have a demonstration. A prototype of future innovation. May I present," she gestured grandly to the device, "the Magisynthesizer."

"Ah," said Thrum. "And what does this hunk of metal do, exactly, Miss…" He glanced at the paper in front of him. "Margarine?"

Margot sighed. "Marsgrøldæg," she corrected, wincing. "But please, just call me Margot."

"Well, I certainly can't be expected to pronounce these ethnic names, Miss Marbledarg," the wizard said. "You'll just have to make do with my best attempt."

"Mar-go," Margot pronounced slowly. "Just… *Mar-go.*"

"Miss Marmalade, please! Can't you just get on with it already?"

Margot clenched her jaw. "Very well. To answer your question, what my machine does," she paused for dramatic effect, "is cast spells!"

There was a flat silence throughout the room.

"Oh, I can do that," said one of the wizards.

"So can I," said another.

"Me too," confessed yet another.

They could no longer maintain straight faces and fell to guffaws. When wizards of a certain rank laughed, they only ever guffawed, although they did occasionally deign to chortle.

"Yes, all joking aside, Miss Margramblegarg," the department head said, stymying his chortles, "what precisely is the point of this device?"

"Why," said Margot, "it is synthetic, mechanized spellcasting! I have used nothing but pure dwarven science to do magic! It's only very simple for now, of course, but it's a proof of concept, and…"

The wizards were checking their wrist-crystals and glancing longingly at the door. Margot's words died in her throat, her confidence rapidly draining away. She made terrified eye contact with Galloway. He gave her a nervous thumbs-up and a horsey grin.

"I'll just demonstrate, how about?" she said cheerfully and turned to her device.

She powered it up. It was supposed to be something small at first, just sparks. The power supply likely wouldn't be able to handle anything much more than that. But though she wasn't facing them now, she kept seeing the department head's smirk, the wizards' eyerolls, their *chortles*. The lowest setting on the device would produce a simple orb of light, which would then fade away.

She could hear it already. 'Oh, it's a fun little box that makes light! How quaint!'

She heard the distant beginnings of another wretched chortle.

No. This was supposed to make a *statement*. She couldn't make a statement if what she did wasn't genuinely impressive.

She cranked the settings all the way up, programming a series of displays.

"Observe," she said brightly, and slammed her fist on the big red button, which she had installed specifically so she could slam it.

The Magisynthesizer began to whirr loudly, heating up. It's production node lit up. Then, in a bright shaft of light, a pure-white unicorn with a pink mane and little hearts on its rump appeared several feet above the floor. Its eyes rolled wildly as gravity took over, its legs flailing in the second it took for it to fall to the ground—immediately it was off like a lightning bolt, leaping directly through the window to escape, promptly falling to its death in the clouds.

Galloway whinnied in startled terror. A couple of brownies shuffled out of their brownie-holes to clean up the broken glass, muttering angrily about inconsiderate students.

"A unicorn-maker," Thrum said. "How quaint. Miss Marblecake, what is the point of this?"

"The point!?" sputtered Margot. "This was advanced apparition! A complex, living being, conjured from thin air! This is *astonishing!*"

"Miss Marzipan," he said, slowly as though explaining something to someone extremely dim. "Any first-year student can manage a complex apparition. Surely you haven't spent six years doing this? Although," he sighed, "I suppose, with your dwarven heritage, it is only what can be expected."

"I know that any first-year student can do that," Margot said hotly. "The point is I made a machine that does it by *itself.* If you would just let me explain my research…"

Thrum tapped his fingers on the table.

"No, wait," Margot said desperately. "Let me show you one more thing first."

This time when she calibrated the machine, all she could imagine was the notion that all her work would be rejected on the opinion of one infuriating, narrow-minded man. She couldn't let that happen. She wouldn't.

The settings were all at maximum, the most advanced file loaded. She hadn't quite finished working out the bugs in this one, but those were just surface details. The core essentials were correct. She'd remembered checking them last week, in the middle of the night, after her fourth cup of dragonfire...

She slammed the big red button. Again, the Magisynthesizer began to whirr. And then, it continued to whirr. In fact, it whirred louder. It also hazarded a clunk, and then two clunks, and then a troubling array of internal ricochets. But its mere sounds were not the trouble—it was certainly the smells that were the worst of it. Specifically, the smell of smoke and battery acid and burning rubber.

The wizards were sitting and watching with faint interest. "Force fields!" Margot shrieked, and jumped clear.

The Magisynthesizer did not so much explode as dissociate completely. The air around it began to distort and waver, popping with sickly blooms of light and grating low-frequency sound. Parts of it blinked in and out of reality. Finally, with a wet ripping sound it simply...disappeared.

There was nothing left of it but an embarrassing scorch mark on the floor.

Galloway hesitantly spoke up. "I thought it was pretty good," he said with an uncertain cheer.

Margot slowly surveyed the scene. She straightened to her full, modest height and returned to the center of the stage. She cleared her throat and took her notecards out of her sleeve.

"And now," she said, "for the verbal presentation portion of my work."

Thrum sighed, extinguishing a small flame which had ignited the tip of his beard. "That, Miss Marbles," he said, "will not be necessary."

FOUR

THE LOCAL CANTINA WAS a place of cheap booze, under-the-table deals for study drugs, and lousy atmosphere. It was too loud, too crowded, and always smelled terrible. Nobody had received remotely respectable service there in centuries. The cocktails were as likely to poison you as to merely intoxicate you, and a minimum of one felony was committed there each weekend. It was located low in Arcana's atmosphere, far below the glittering academic buildings, where the gravity was heavy and the lamentations heavier.

It was, of course, wildly popular.

It was there that Margot sat on the too-tall barstool, sipping her drink, hoping vaguely to drown in it.

"And another thing," she hiccupped, "string theory? Complete unicorn crap! It's fundamentally not a realist viewpoint! Sure, the math is beautiful, but so what?"

"I understand and agree completely," said the

young wizard on the barstool beside her, who clearly had not understood anything in his entire life, let alone anything Margot had said to him. "Can I buy you another drink?"

"Please," Margot said, shoving her empty glass of lichenbrew across the countertop. "And y'know what else I hate? Emergence."

"That's really interesting," said the wizard. "Have I told you that I'm really into dwarves?"

"Three times now," Margot confirmed absently. She took out a few salvaged mechanical and electrical components from her pocket and aimlessly started fiddling with them. "I mean, what kind of nonsense is that, *emergence?* It's an empty buzzword!"

"I sympathize with you," the graduate wizard said. "And I really like your stumpy legs. Is it true that dwarf women grow beards?"

Margot knocked back the rest of her fifth lichenbrew. "Thanks," she sniffled. "You're a great listener."

Margot blearily stared at the mirror hanging in the upper corner of the room. It had interrupted the comet race being televised to deliver a special report about a fairy terrorist being spotted in the western spiral arm of the neighboring galaxy, with the scroll text reminding viewers to be on the watch for some escaped goblin criminal. Oh, as though she cared.

This was, she thought, the absolute worst possible thing that could have happened to her.

Functionally forced out of the Academy. Her work made a mockery of. Her years of effort, wasted. What was she going to do? Where was she going to go?

Oh, sweet starlight, what would her mother say?

She could just imagine it already. The passive-aggressive jibes. The implicit *I-told-you-so's*. The home-cooked family dinner, made with pure spite. The sweet, homey smiles laced with self-satisfaction. The assurances of her family, agreeing that while she had been extremely stupid, they would continue to love her and were ready to welcome her back into the fold. The inevitable offer of a job at her mother's space station.

Margot was shaken out of her reverie by a sudden magical duel breaking out in the corner. Neither participants' aim was much good at their present level of intoxication, however, and a stray bolt of bright green energy streaked across the room and hit the graduate wizard square in the back, turning him into a frog.

"Hey," Margot complained loudly. "He was buying me drinks."

The students who had been dueling looked over to her.

"Hey," one of them said. "Isn't that the Academy's most down-to-ground student?"

"Oh, honestly. Short jokes?" Margot growled as the graduate frog hopped madly up and down on the bar stool. "*Real* original."

"Woah," another of them said. "Don't blow your short-fuse, huh?"

They fell to guffawing. Margot fumed, returning to her drink. How could news of her failure have spread so quickly?

At that moment, Fabiocious Galloway entered the room, by falling into it from the second floor. He was clearly already plastered—though mostly from the plaster in the ceiling he'd just fallen through. The bar scene briefly fell quiet to note his arrival, and then returned to their conversations.

"Hello Professor Galloway," Margot said moodily. She continued fiddling with the little device she'd been constructing as she drank. Maybe it'd be a portable death ray. Maybe that would make her feel better.

"Tough break today kid," Galloway said. "I'm real sorry about it. Hey, you haven't seen a goblin around here, have you?"

"It's okay," said Margot, angrily setting one of
the amplification crystals she kept on her person into
the device. "Actually, no. It's not remotely okay. It's
completely disastrous."

"Because, see," Galloway said, "this goblin, I owe
him money. He's been coming after me for a while and
I'm just a bit short on cash right now, and seeing as he's
out of jail, I might be in serious trouble this time."

"But you know what the worst thing is?" Margot
said.

"And y'know…they're gonna say that I'm not a
real centaur for not just suing him, or at least giving him
a good trample, but I'm just not that kinda guy. I like
being around humans. They're so relaxed. They never
did anything like invent social media." Galloway
shuddered. "I hate social media. That stuff's an anxiety
machine."

"The worst thing is that it doesn't even matter
that it blew up!" Margot slammed her fist on the table.
"The problem is that I have no idea *why* it blew up!
None of my models remotely predicted this happening!
Science is supposed to be about *understanding*. And I
didn't understand anything about what happened
today! You know what that means?"

"And this goblin...he's just, a rude guy, y'know? And I don't really wanna deal with him. So if you see a goblin around, tell him the centaur-shaped hole in the ceiling wasn't me."

"It means that all my work has been a waste. Everything I thought I knew? It's bupkis. Poppycock. Worthless twaddle. I'm going to have to start all over again, from my most basic hypotheses. And I'm going to have to do it without Academy funding."

Galloway finally picked himself off the floor, awkwardly lurching up and clopping over to the bar. He ordered a large boot-shaped glass container of something pink and a silly straw.

"But yeah," he said. "Really sucks about today. Uh, I'm guessing you failed?"

"Yes, Professor Galloway."

"Right, right...I wasn't sure, cause I really liked it! I thought it was great! Just absolutely fantastic! Couldn't be prouder of you! And then I tuned out for the rest of the committee meeting because I know *Divorce Court's Next Top Model* is always on around this time and I just couldn't get my mind off it. But you seemed pretty upset afterwards so I figured the news wasn't good."

"No, Professor Galloway."

"Damn. Yeah. Sucks."

"Sucks," Margot said. "Yes, it certainly sucks, how I'm a complete failure as both a wizard *and* a dwarf. It assuredly *sucks* that my dream is dead and my heart is broken."

Galloway shrugged, sipping on his silly straw. "That's alright. I'm a complete failure as both a centaur and a professor, and I somehow manage to get by. I watch my TV shows and I drink my beers. Life is okay."

Margot sighed heavily. TV shows and beers. Getting by. "At least we can be failures together."

Galloway lifted his drink. "To failure!" he declared.

"To failure," Margot resigned.

They drank.

At that moment, something which might have been an extremely overgrown and toothy amphibian of a sickly orange color slammed open the double doors.

"Hey, you!" the goblin shouted, pointing at Galloway. "You horse's ass, you owe me money!"

Galloway dropped his drink in shock. "I, uh," he whinnied. "I'm real sorry, fella, I just don't have—"

"Don't give me any of that space junk, you crunk!" the goblin growled, and pulled a wand with clear murderous intent. "You horse's ass, I've had it with your cantering ways, so today, once and for all, I'm gonna do away—"

Margot flipped the switch on the portable death ray she'd been building. Immediately the bar filled with violet light, engulfing the snarling goblin in an intolerable radiance. All of a sudden, he turned into a swarm of rainbow butterflies, which scattered across the room, out the door and through the windows.

"Aw, geez," Margot muttered. "That was *supposed* to vaporize him. Why doesn't this darn magic make any danged sense? Ugh!"

She noticed the sudden silence, the stares. She glared around, lifting her defective death ray again. "And if anyone else wants to shout any more racial slurs at my friends," she announced, "or, for that matter, make any short jokes, there's plenty more where that came from!"

There was a brief silence. Then the cantina band went back to its playing and everyone returned to their drinks.

Galloway was visibly shaken. "Another gargleblaster please," he said woozily to the bartender. "Margot, you didn't have to do that. I mean, he totally would have killed me, but...sometimes I almost think I'd be better off that way." He cast his gaze downwards. "I'm not really much use to anyone. I wasn't to you."

Margot sighed and hopped down from the bar stool. She patted his flank. "It's okay, Professor Galloway. You did your best." She pocketed her defective death ray. "I mean, your best was utterly subpar, but you tried, and that's what matters."

She made for the door. She didn't want to spend any more money drinking. Passage back to Duluth-9 would be pricey, and she'd be catching the first ship home at daybreak.

At least at home there would be hotdish.

As she slummed her way down the street back to the inn where she'd be staying her final night in the carbon clouds of Arcana, she heard a faint tinkling.

"Hey," a voice said. Margot turned. It was a pixie, or maybe a fairy—Margot could never tell them apart—hovering cheerfully at eye level not too far from her. Her dark skin glowed slightly violet, her cyan hair styled in an updo.

"Oh," said Margot. "Hello."

"I saw what you did in there," the pixie said. "Real good of you, standing up for that centaur."

Margot shrugged. "It was nothing. He was my friend."

"Nothing? You're a hero! You totally wrecked the guy with that little thingie!" the pixie said. "What is it, some newfangled kinda wand?"

"No, it's a death ray," Margot explained. "I built it, but it doesn't even work. It was supposed to vaporize him into dust, not turn him into butterflies. The problems of being the sole developer of magitech, I guess."

"You built that?" the pixie asked, awed, her bubblegum eyes wide. "Wow! I'm really impressed."

"Yeah," Margot said. "I guess it is pretty impressive, even if it didn't work. It's just science, though."

"Well, hey, he's dead, right? Seems pretty powerful to me."

"I guess...although, I think he might just be alive as a swarm of butterflies now. Maybe he'll get in less trouble this way."

The pixie giggled. "Hey, you're pretty cute," she said, hovering closer. "I'm Lyxie."

"I'm Margot. Yeah, uh...you're not so bad yourself."

Margot's heart raced. She had a historically bad track record with women. She always ended up talking too much about her work, or talking too much in general. *Being* too much.

Margot had always been too much.

"You want we should go back to your place? So you can show me some more of your death rays?"

"I..." Margot hesitated. This wasn't really like her. But, she'd been drinking, and she'd had an awful day. She'd had six years of the endless academic grind, of never having the time for herself, of never doing anything fun. Maybe she could allow this. Just one single nice memory before she returned home to her mother's smugness and a lifetime of getting by. "You know what? Sure. Sounds peachy to me. Let's go."

Lyxie giggled, twining an arm through hers. "You're funny," she said. "Tell me more about this science stuff."

FIVE

MARGOT AWOKE THE NEXT morning at the inn, bleary and tangled in the sweaty sheets. She had a splitting hangover and a sinking feeling.

She sat up, blinking. Roiling clouds outside. Bare walls. Bare carpets. Clothes scattered across the floor.

There was something wrong here, and she couldn't quite tell what it was.

She got up, pulling on yesterday's clothes in a fog. Crystal ball on the nightstand. Empty bottles on the floor. Pain behind her eyes.

She walked around the room a few times, mystified. She wandered into the bathroom. Toothbrush. Razor, an old-fashioned dwarven one made of metal and not one of those magical ones— those always made her nervous. What was her wristwatch doing in the tub?

She wandered out of the bathroom, aimlessly looking around for her duffel with all her things in it. That was odd. She could have sworn she'd left it by the bed, right before the pixie had...

"Ah," she said aloud, because it felt better than having to suffer through the realization in silence. "It appears that the pixie took advantage of my vulnerable state and robbed me."

Margot crossed her arms, rocking from foot to foot. "Why, I'd venture a guess that she was misleading me right from the start, feigning scientific interest in my work just to steal it. It seems I've been conned, gentlemen. Bamboozled. Made victim of a tomfool's chicanery."

She was only part way through all her synonyms for 'conned' when the cleaning ogre threw her out of the room and onto the street, with nothing to her name but a toothbrush, a razor, and a priceless unique marvel of technology.

Well, Margot thought, quite calmly. This was it. Stranded on a student moon without a penny to her name, the past six years of effort wasted. No place to stay, no way to get home. No steadfast friends. This really was rock bottom at last. Not even rock bottom. Magma bottom. Hot iron core bottom. Superconducting metallic hydrogen bottom. If someone had deigned to hand her a shovel, it would have been crushed under the enormous hydrostatic pressure.

This was it.

With nowhere to go and no idea what to do, Margot shoved her hands deep in her pockets and started walking.

She wandered through the streets of lower Arcana, halfway considering simply sitting down and begging, before remembering that this was a student planet and nobody here had any money anyway. She considered armed robbery—but with what? Her razor? She didn't even have her malfunctioning death ray anymore.She might have actually tried it, except that afternoon a desperate freshman jumped her as she tried to shave in a storefront window, and stole that too. Which, she felt, was still not as ridiculous as having her toothbrush plucked out of her hand by a passing bird and then immediately dropped into the sewers.

Just as the sun was setting and Margot sat down on the curb to have herself a complete emotional breakdown followed by a good long cry, her wristwatch buzzed. At least the pixie had only taken her death ray and not her watch. Margot's mother was calling her. She sighed and answered. If anything was a sign, this was it.

"Hey there, sweetie," her mother's voice crackled through.

"Hi, Mom."

"Just wondering how you were doin', honey. You never call! How's all that doofy magic stuff working out? How are you doing? You're not in any trouble, are ya?"

"Oh, it's…" Margot stared into the middle distance. She opened her mouth, and then closed it. "Really great, actually. Yeah, fantastic. I just had a big breakthrough, and I think I'm going to be pretty busy on it for a while."

"Oh, yeah? Well, good for you, honey. I was gonna hassle you to come by and visit, but geez, if you're too busy to even visit your poor old mom, then I guess I can't stop you from being too good for us, huh?"

"I guess so!" Margot said tightly.

"Aw, I'm just joshin' you sweetie. You know we love you. And you can come home any time you want, okay? I'll make your favorite hotdish, special for you. We can get the whole family together, maybe talk about your future. I just had an opening for an engineer over at the station, and I was just thinking, if you weren't sure where to go from here, you could come work for me for a while."

"That won't be necessary," Margot said. "Y'know, this breakthrough, it's a pretty big deal, actually. I'd tell you more about it, but I doubt you'd want to hear about doofy magic stuff, right?"

"Oh, hon, no need for that," her mother said sweetly. "Well, like ya said, you're probably pretty busy, so this old bat will go ahead and leave you alone. You take care of yourself now."

"Thanks, Mom. Bye."

The wristwatch went quiet.

Margot stared at it, feeling oddly at peace.

Suddenly, she was filled with resolve.

There was just something about absolute despair (and conversations with her mother) which did the trick.

Actually, Margot thought, getting to her feet, she *wasn't* going to go home. And not just because she didn't have the money for passage. She wasn't going home because she wasn't going to abandon her research. She wasn't going to bow to her mother's whims. And she *certainly* wasn't going to give up.

She glared upward through the clouds, behind which she knew would be the vast expanse of space. She was going to find some way off this rock. She was going to rebuild her Magisynthesizer better than ever. She was going to *show* everyone who had ever doubted her. She was going to tear the universe apart, down to its tiniest fundamental particle, and she was going to find out how magic worked. She was going to *win*.

But first, she was going to steal herself some new shoes, because the pixie had taken those, too.

A FICTION VORTEX SERIES

My Fair Dragon

tail as old as time

Camille Kietzman

MY FAIR DRAGON

CAMILLE KIETZMAN

Episode 1: Pinocchio

One

ASTEROID Z-186 WAS small and cold, even for an asteroid. Its atmosphere was thin and its surface toxic to humans. It was poisonous enough to kill someone in five minutes, Father explained. He pulled out charts and graphs to demonstrate it to her, hanging them up and whapping them with sticks. She clapped right away, prompting Father to hush her.

"Silence, child," he said. "I have not even begun my lecture."

"Oh!" Mathildax covered her mouth. "There's a lecture? I want to hear it!"

Father was too smart for her to understand, but she still listened raptly, staring at the charts. She did like the charts. They were so colorful and pretty, and the pictures moved. Father had said one day he would teach her to enchant pictures if she were smart enough, but for now all she could do was look at them.

"…and within the second layer beneath the asteroid's surface, the essence of lost souls, fused to form the most deadly—child, are you listening?"

"Oh yes!" Mathildax said. "Deadly. Poisonous. Pretty colors."

Father frowned, and tugged on his goatee. "You must pay attention, child. Your ability to focus and retain information is an important part of—what did I say about licking things?"

"Mrrrgh?" Mathildax asked, her tongue already lapping against the board. Father scrunched his nose and started to gently guide her away from the board.

"I said," he repeated testily, "Do not! Lick! The board! Or anything else, for that matter!"

"Yeah!" interjected an image on the board. It was a picture of one of the green, gnarly faces roiling under the drawn surface of the asteroid. "Don't lick things!"

"Silence!" Father told it, waving his hand at it right as Mathildax withdrew her tongue. "Now, onto the next slide."

That had been when her head only came up to

Father's knee. Each new time he gave the lecture, she was a little taller and could remember more. Like how Z-186 had been declared "completely uninhabitable." Or all the names of the various deadly substances on the asteroid. Or how Father's ingenious enchanted robe allowed him to live here without immediately shriveling up, and how he had to cast spells upon them every day with meticulous detail.

Now the tips of her horns reached his neck when she stood tall and straight on her back legs. She rolled over on her side this time, fixing her eyes on the swirling charts and frowning.

"Father," she said. "If our asteroid is small, then what is big?"

Father stopped, staring for a moment.

"Also," she continued, "if this place is cold, then what place is warm? And, and…if its atmosphere is poisonous to humans and its surface all deadly and everything so that people can't walk on it except with the robe you created, because humans were not meant to walk here—"

"Fewer words, child."

"Then," she said impatiently, swishing her tail, "where were humans made to walk? And where are all the other humans, anyway?"

Father looked at her, the corners of his mouth tugging downwards. Before he could answer, one of the chairs piped up, jumping up and down with excitement.

"The planets!" it said. "Tell her about the planets!"

"Yeah!" A stray, mangled plant spoke up. "Tell her about them!"

"Silence, minions!" Father hissed. They piped down, whining as they did so. "The planets...human society...I have dreaded the day this subject would arise."

"But," Mathildax said. "But..."

Father gave a great wave of his staff, expertly dismissing all of his slides. "There are other planets. Planets that dwarf our tiny home. Planets close to the stars. Planets warm and full of clear air. And they teem with life and other experimental resources. But they are filled with..." his face darkened, "People."

"People, oh no!" Mathildax gasped. Then, she paused, tilting her head. "Wait, aren't we people? What's so bad about people?"

Father's face pulled into a deep frown. "It is best," he said wisely (like the wise old sage he was), "that you never find out."

TWO

MATHILDAX HAD RUN ALL the way around the surface of Z-186 two hundred and six times since she had started counting. She had talked to every oozing growth on the side of the mountains, every twisted and moaning rock, every chattering appliance in Father's laboratory. She had dug her way through every slimy green cave she could find. There was simply nothing left to do.

"It's not that I'm ungrateful," she said, resting her head on her forearms as she looked out to the stars. They shone every hour of her existence, billions of miles away, but still comforting her. "I am. Father is a wonderful, intelligent mage like he says, and I have everything I could ever want. It's only…"

The bubbling growth on the side of the mountain hissed.

"I know, I know," she sighed. "But I want to see more of the cosmos! What is 'big' and 'warm' like, anyway? What are the people out there all like? They can't all be bad."

The growth gave a distinctly sympathetic sounding gurgle.

"Maybe I—but no, I shouldn't."

"*Mrrp?*" it asked.

"I mean," she said. "There are so many rooms that are locked to me…I'm sure in some of them there's more information about all these places. But I couldn't."

The bubbling became insistent.

"Don't give me that," she sighed, rolling over to look at it. "I'm not giving up. I just don't want Father to be mad at me, is all."

More bubbling and hissing.

"Well, I bet I couldn't, even if I tried," she huffed. "Father's so careful, I bet all the doors are extra enchanted! The doors are probably sealed shut with the strongest magic: unbreakable, unfireable, and—"

THREE

THE DOORS WERE NOT, as it turned out, enchanted nearly so well. In fact one broke with a single hard knock.

"Oh dear," she whimpered.

"Trouble! Trouble! You're in trouble!" the door said.

"I didn't expect it to work! Be quiet."

She stepped into the room. There were shelves of books, flasks, wands, staves, and in the center, a mirror as tall as she was. It glistened, light shimmering off its surface—a remarkable feat, considering there was almost no light in there. She crept up to it, and saw some distinctly lickable color manifest in it. She reached out her hands, transfixed.

"You shouldn't," warned the door.

"I shouldn't," Mathildax repeated.

But she grabbed the mirror, grabbed several books with interesting pictures on the cover, and fled to her room. She shut away any pencil or books that started to hiss and shout what she'd done. She rolled up one poster on the wall that hollered at her to stop and take everything back.

Finally, she looked in the mirror.

Images swirled within it. She saw mysterious spheres orbiting the stars, their surfaces all layered with different colors. Hunks of carved steel sailed through the stars, faces peeking out their windows. Then, brightness. So, so much brightness, followed by lines of people in robes, their hands sparkling as they circled around a fire, swaying to and fro.

"Human society!" Mathildax gasped.

She touched her thick, hard fingers to the mirror and swiped it. Each new swipe brought a different image: a blue atmosphere with wispy shapes floating around it, water that poured in abundance without being squeezed from rocks, and fields of rippling grass. The people she saw—such magic they had! They made hunks of rock sail through the sky, and had devices that made water swirl down little tubes.

Knowing that Father would find her any moment, she locked her door and stared deeply into the glass.

Four

WHEN FATHER BURST IN—approximately four hours later—he immediately began wailing.

"After all I have done," he said. "You go behind my back like this?"

Mathildax curled up, her wings wrapping around her protectively. "But…I wanted to see more!'

Father's face crumbled. He paced. "Of course you did," he sighed. "Bright, inquisitive, so full of wonder and curiosity…you get it from my side of the family." He paused, considering his own wisdom. "As you do not have any other side, that is. But child, the cosmos is a dark and cruel place, full of darkness! And cruelty!"

"But," Mathildax held up her mirror, "they have pretty buildings! And sparkly bath potions that light up! And they make their water *swirl!*" Surely, she thought, any people that had those delightful devices of swirling liquid could not be all bad.

Father's face darkened. "It does not matter," he

said. "Humans are foul and corrupt, and they will crush you underfoot! If only you knew of the wrongs…the persecution…"

Mathildax remembered the definition of "persecution" from her last vocabulary lesson. She nodded, and Father continued.

"Humans stamp out any innocence they see," he told her, still pacing. "They sort through themselves as children. They find soft ones, the weak ones, and do you know what they do to them?"

She tensed, an anxious shudder running down her tail. "What do they do, Father?"

"They shove them into lockers!" Father said. "They mock them with names such as 'nerd' and 'dweeb'!"

"Oh no!" Mathildax cried, clutching one of her pillows. "What is a 'nerd'?"

Father didn't respond, already in a frenzy. "And they smother any experimental advancement, any spark of ingenuity or invention!" he cried. "They are herd animals, clawing someone back down the moment genius has elevated them. The moment one has a breakthrough, you are immediately slandered!"

"Slandered?" Mathildax asked, wondering what the word meant.

Father continued over her, muttering. "'Unethical' they said. 'Immoral' they said. 'You can't just infuse sentience into every object you find,' they said. Well, I showed them!"

"Yeah!" a crack in the wall cried out in agreement. "You showed them!"

"And then they stop inviting you to Guild parties!" Father wailed. "They call you a madman! A madman!"

"That's so unfair," Mathildax said. She didn't understand, but if Father was this upset, it must have been *terrible* for him. Tears began to well in her eyes.

"Mind your tears, child," he said. "I just repaired the furniture in this room. We don't want the acid getting everywhere again."

She sniffled, wiping her eyes. A few stray drops hit the floor and sizzled, creating burn marks where they landed. Meanwhile, Father took a few deep breaths, calming down until he slumped.

"I suppose I cannot keep you safe from the truth of things forever," he sighed finally. "Such a bright, inquisitive child, so much like myself. Very well. You make look through all the information I have locked away about the worlds humans dwell in."

Mathildax shot up. "You mean it?" she cried.

"Yes," he said sadly. "If it is what you want."

She leapt forward and hugged him, causing him to wheeze painfully.

"Oh, thank you!" she said. "Thank you so much!"

FIVE

SHE LOOKED INTO THE mirror for hours, read every book she could get her hands on. She read them lying down, sitting up, walking around Z-186. She learned about human schools, human festivals, human playgrounds—all the wonderful things there were on other planets inhabited by humans.

She didn't keep track of time as she devoured each new book. She hardly noticed as day after day more spikes sprouted along her spine, her tail lengthened, and the height of her head slowly crept up to Father's. She kept walking around Z-186 until she'd circled it three hundred times, four hundred times— and then stopped bothering to count. Soon she'd read every book twice, and all amused her were the bright images of other worlds in her mirror.

"I just wish," she sighed. "I could see it all for myself."

"See it all for yourself," the window agreed faintly.

Father's hair had gone white, all sorts of new lines sprouting around his eyes. He didn't move around so much anymore. He stayed in the lab and left collecting new materials to her. Soon he conducted his research entirely from his bed, and rested more and more.

One day, lying in bed, he told her about a shuttle that he had docked under the lab. A vessel, he said in a shaky voice, which would take her to the nearest planet when she was ready to leave. His eyes watered as he explained all the necessary spells to direct it.

"But stay a little longer," he told her. "There is so much knowledge to impart to you, so much of my research. I have so little time…"

Six

SHE WALKED AROUND THE asteroid again. All of the normally babbling vegetation was unusually quiet.

"Do you think he'll be sad when I leave?"

Normally something would have answered immediately, but this time there was solemn silence. Finally, something spoke up.

"Leave…" It was a crater.

"Oh, you think so too?" she asked. "But Father might be lonely…"

"Lonely," it said.

"It will be hard to say goodbye."

"Good…bye…"

Eventually, she summoned up her courage and burst into Father's room, breaking the doors off the hinges as she did so.

"Father," she said. "I want to leave now. I need to go out and explore the cosmos. I need to meet other humans!"

Father was silent, not even deigning to move a

finger. He was slumped, his head rolled to the side at an awkward angle. She wondered if he was asleep, but he couldn't be. His eyes were still wide open.

"If…if you don't want me to go, then say so," she said.

Father said nothing.

"You're alright with it?" she asked. "Are you sure? Do you have anything to say against it?"

Father voiced no objection at all. After waiting a moment, she jumped up and down.

"Oh goodie!" she said. "Thank you so much! I'll head off immediately then!"

She darted off, her tail spikes whipping hard enough against the door to dent it on the way out. She bolted through the hallway and right into the room with the ship, before stopping dead in her tracks.

"Oh wait!" she said. "I have to pack first."

Nothing in the house answered her. She bolted back down the hall.

"I'll have to take all the books. And I couldn't leave my posters, my blanket, the shelves, or the burning slime, or—oh wait! I need a place to put everything! Father?"

Luckily Father had several enchanted storage devices. She opened one and started to pack, mostly by throwing everything at the object and watching as it sucked everything up. She tossed in the cobwebs and dust as an afterthought, because she felt sorry for them.

"I don't want you to stay behind," she said. "That would be really lonely! To have to stay here by yourselves after being with all the others for so long."

She blinked. Stinging tears were forming at the corners of her eyes.

"Oh," she said. "I'm leaving him all alone now. I'm a terrible daughter, aren't I?"

When nothing, not even the walls, answered, she rushed back into Father's room. He hadn't moved since she'd last seen him, not at all.

"Father," she sniffled. "I just wanted to say you're the greatest wizard ever, and the best father! And you've done so much for me. Thank you."

She wished he would say something, but when he was quiet for another minute, she realized he must want rest.

"Well," she said. "Goodbye. I'll come back! And I'll write every day!"

She glanced back once. Father's eyes were still wide, still gazing up at the ceiling. She turned and left, making her rounds.

"Goodbye chairs! And other chairs!" she said.

"Goodbye cracked window, weird yellow window, brown window. Goodbye shrieking plants, and craters, and endless energy of lost souls beneath the surface! Thank you for everything!"

She tried to get everyone, every single object that had ever said a word to her, and a few of the ones who never managed more than a gurgle now and then. She wished they would say something back—waited for them too as she got the ship ready. Finally, after she had packed her storage cubicle and was ready to leave, she stood in the doorway for a few minutes.

"Does anyone have anything to say?"

They didn't. "Well, goodbye again!" she said brightly. "Goodbye, and thanks for everything!"

With that, she launched the ship.

SEVEN

THE SHIP HAD A single window, small and musty, but still enough for her to see out of as the nearest human planet came into view. She paced with excitement, and licked it in anticipation. Soon it was close enough for her to gape at an assortment of moons and stars hanging in a purple sky. As the ship lowered, she saw neat rows of purple that turned into a detailed array of leaves. Farm crops, she realized. A magic fed crop she had seen pictures of in her books.

"Ooh, exciting!" she chirped. "It's so much brighter than in the books! It's so—"

The ship collided with the ground before she could finish her sentence. She shrieked as the crash made her slam into the ceiling, and then the floor. Dizzily, she pulled herself up and made for the exit. She heard something outside, muffled words she couldn't quite make out. Rustling. Tentatively, she leaned close to the window again, rubbing at it in an attempt to remove some of the muck that made it hard to see.

Squinting, she could make out some figures running to and fro around the ship. People. Humans.

She burst through the door so fast it went flying off its hinges. She gasped as the atmosphere of the world hit her skin.

"Greetings, fellow humans!" she bellowed.

The humans, all flocked around her ship with wide eyes, jumped back, gasping.

"Dragon!" one screamed. "It's a dragon!"

"Dragon?" Mathildax yelped, despite not knowing what a dragon was. "Where?"

The humans all dispersed, dropping pitchforks and practically climbing over each other as they fled. Mathildax whipped her head around, but saw nothing. In a moment of confusion and panic, she bolted back into the ship and slammed the door shut, screaming at the top of her lungs.

Eight

ONCE SHE WAS PRETTY sure the threat, whatever it had been, had passed, she emerged to start sniffing out the world again. There were so many colors, it hurt her eyes. They were so much closer to their star, and it made everything around her so painfully bright before her eyes adjusted. Once they had, she could focus in on the details. Tiny little green spikes on the ground. Brown cracked growths with green, veiny blossoms. She couldn't do anything but stop and gape for a moment.

She flapped her wings, reaching out her tongue a moment before thinking better of it.

"Hello tree and grass!" she said. "I am Mathildax. I read about you in a book. May I lick you?"

"I'm sorry," she said. "I can't really understand your accent? I'm from off planet. Could you maybe not say anything if you don't want me to lick you, but nod if you are okay with it?"

She waited. Silence, for a while. But then, there

was an air current and the tree was nodding its leaves.
She clapped her hands together.

"Oh goodie! Thank you so much!"

She licked it. It reminded her a bit of the rocks at
home, except warmer and softer. It eroded underneath
her tongue, and when she was done the bark had been
stripped off, laying the lighter wood beneath it bare.
She flapped her wings.

"That was the best I've ever tasted!" she told it.

The grass was the next best thing she ever tasted.
Then the rocks, the water, and the mud. She thanked
them all excitedly, flapping her wings and then rolling
around for a little while. She explained to them all that
the scales all around her made it difficult for her to
know what things felt like unless she licked them.

"I get to taste things and feel them that way!" she
chirped.

The world was oddly silent. Perhaps everyone
here was just shy. Eventually, in the absence of an
answer, she hopped up and continued on.

The humans were even shyer, it turned out. The
human "town" she entered was full of beautiful
buildings with bricks of all different vibrant colors:
brown-brown, red-brown, and brown with a tinge of
green, to name a few. Every single brick looked so

lickable. And lick she did, sometimes licking twice for good measure. Only after a dozen or so licks did she realize there was no human to be found. Not on the streets, not inside the buildings, not even under the rocks she started to lift up as she looked for them. She finally found some by pulling up a heavy trapdoor in the ground.

"Greetings, fellow humans!" she said, whapping her tail against the ground.

Instead of answering, the humans opened their mouths wide, threw their heads back, and let out long shrieks before disappearing into the darkness underground. Mathildax stuck her neck in to follow and almost made it—she was about the size of the other humans that had been in the basement, after all—but got caught because her waist was too wide. Huffing, she wriggled her way out and slumped.

"These humans have strange customs," she said, kicking a stray can with her forepaw. "I didn't read about this in the books."

She sighed, but continued looking. It was a very large world, large enough that she hadn't yet been able to detect the curve of its surface from walking on it. There was a lot to explore that didn't involve people, even in their town. She sniffed around, prying open

some doors with her claws and picking through the
different objects she found. There were clay pots that
broke easily in her hand, thin books that tore right as
she opened them, and in a corner, a tiny box that
glowed with scratching noises emerging from it.

She stepped forward, and touched it. The
moment she did, a voice burst into her ears.

"Warning: Red level disaster alert. Dragon
sighted. Seek shelter immediately. The Latona City
barrier is closing, so teleport..."

"Oh no," she said to the box. "That's terrible."

She had no idea what it was saying, but its tone
indicated that it was something intensely serious.

Without acknowledging her response, it
continued. "...The security force is mobilizing as we
speak. Look for any signs of acidic burns or poison,
especially the withering of crops or any trail of..."

Before she could listen to the rest, a flashing sign
on the wall caught her eye. It showed people dancing
around a fire. She dropped the box, barely noticing as it
shattered on the floor and the voice faded into static.
She hopped right over the pieces and stretched her neck
forward to read the sign.

"The Festival of Three Moons," she said aloud.
"Music, food, parade, and a guest performance from the

Ivory Dagger Troupe. Open to all. Occurs at—oh, that's tonight!"

She thought of the images she's seen in the magic mirror back on Z-186, the sight of people twirling and moving with pure joy. She buzzed excitedly.

"A festival? Tonight?" she hopped. She felt an involuntary twitch, one that ran right down her back and made her usually inactive wings twitch. "Oh, where is it? Latona? What's that? Tell me!"

She grabbed the sign with her claws and it cracked in two. Then, she covered her mouth with her forepaws and batted her wings sheepishly, creeping out before anyone could see her.

NINE

SHE ASKED SOME TREES for directions to Latona,
only for them to stubbornly refuse. Even when she
yelled at them, enunciating clearly in case they had
hearing problems, they were useless. Instead she
ambled around aimlessly for a while before she spotted
the misty spires of a city in the distance, their tops
obscured by clouds. She flapped her wings excited and
trotted toward the city as fast as she could.

When she arrived, she found it was a collection
of stone spires that shone and glimmered different
colors in the distance. She stuck her tongue out, ready
to lick every colorful stone in the place. And even
better, as she got closer she noticed there were actual
humans, unlike the last place. They didn't run like the
few she'd encountered so far, but stood in a line right in
front of the entrance of the city, holding staves and
raising them to the sky. She pranced forward excitedly.

"Hello, fellow humans!" she said. "I am—"

Her nose hit an invisible wall before she could

finish her introduction. A solid, burning wall that left her nose stinging.

"Ouch!" she cried, clutching her nose.

A crackle of blue magic flashed before her eyes. A barrier, she realized, just like the ones Father used to put up around their house whenever a new volcano erupted nearby. The crackle faded, leaving the barrier invisible once more. Some of the humans had quavered the moment she had hit the barrier, and were shaking now.

"Keep up the barrier!" one of them shouted, one wearing differently colored robes. "No dragons will ever touch our city again!"

"Owwwww," Mathildax repeated, her eyes still stinging. "What's the barrier for?"

Some of the humans gasped, others flinched. More humans rushed behind the first line, holding their staves tensely. All eyes were on her, and her scales ruffled nervously.

"Um," she said. "Hello, fellow humans. I'm Mathildax. Pleased to meet you all."

There were more, louder gasps. "It talks?" the leader squeaked. "What sort of unholy—? Lieutenant. Call for backup."

Mathildax folded her wings neatly behind her

back. "I don't understand what you mean. Can I come in?"

"Silence," the leader said. "Men, destroy this creature at once!"

"I...what?" Mathildax blinked.

A blast of magic sailed at her face. She shrieked and ducked, letting it pass over her head.

"Hey!" she protested. "That could have hurt! I don't know what you're doing, but I'm standing right here and...ow!"

The next blast of magic hit her in the shoulder.

"Mages!" the leader called. "Give it your all. That barely damaged it!"

"Stop," Mathildax said, not liking how they were ignoring her and also shouting. "I really need to get in now. How am I supposed to get in when you keep this barrier up?"

And then, one of the mages closest to her through the barrier piped up.

"Shut up! *You're* what we're keeping out, you brute! And there's no way we're letting you past this barrier."

She stood blinking, trying to process this. "You're trying to...but...but how will you get to like me if you never let me in?"

The response she got was a huge blast, one too fast to dodge in time. It blew her off her feet and right into a tree, which snapped under the force of her weight. She scrambled up, disoriented.

"Fine!" she said, feeling her eye prickle. "Fine. *Be that way!*"

But somehow instead of the words coming out, all that came out was a splutter of flame that dispersed and hit the grass. Embarrassed, she ran off, tears prickling at her eyes.

TEN

THEY CHASED HER THROUGH the woods, right until she hit a giant wall. Once she had rammed her nose in it and yelped, she took a brief step back to look at what she had run into. The giant wall stretched in front of her, the words "DANGER, GO NO FURTHER," and, "EVIL LIES HERE" scrawled across it in large red letters, repeating again and again to cover as much of the wall as possible. Before she could process the implications of this though, she heard the humans trampling closer behind her.

Panicked, she jumped the wall, quickly figuring that it would be better than running along it. She expected to drop to the ground on the other side, but instead she fell through dark obscuring mist. She flailed, and found herself plummeting to the bottom of an enormous pit.

She was afraid of heights, she realized in that moment.

"Father!" she cried. Or at least, that's what she

instinctively attempted to blurt out. The result sounded more like

"FATHEEEEEREEAAAAAAAAAAAAAAAAAAAAAAAA AAAAAAAK."

It hurt when she landed, but she got up, sniffling. More tears threatened to fall, and she rubbed her eyes to stop them.

Far, far above, she heard some shouts. The humans were still looking for her. At least they couldn't see her anymore. Not with the wall, or the obscuring mist over the top. As far away as the top was, though, she could still strain her ears to faintly make out some of their conversation.

"The Pit!"

"We can't go down there, down there is the—!"

"Sir, you can't possibly make us—"

"Silence!"

A hush fell over all of them. A voice spoke up, a bit louder and stronger than the others had been.

"We will return and report our mission was a success," the voice said. "Nothing comes out of there alive. Not even dragons. Leave it, and the problem will take care of itself."

There were a few shouts of joy, and the sound of trampling footsteps fading into the distance. She listened until she could no longer hear even the slightest traces of their conversation, and then she snapped her tail against the ground.

"Meanies!" she bellowed after them.

Once the echo of her voice died, she curled up, buried her face in her hands, and wailed.

Greetings from the Authors

IF YOU HAVE GOTTEN THIS far, hopefully you are looking forward to reading more of *Wizards in Space* and other Fiction Vortex™ StoryVerses™. You're in luck! We have an official butt-load of episodes available. Check out our mobile app, www.fictionite.io, for copious FREE episodes and more.

Fiction Vortex is all about episodic fiction like the stuff you just read. We are boiling with excitement over how many people have jumped into the Vortex along with us. Thus far, our StoryVerses™ have been a crazy stupid success, but our baby is still so young and frail!

It's time to suckle the milk of brilliant genre fiction until our bones grow strong enough to withstand the slings and arrows of traditional publishing's lumbering giant. At Fiction Vortex™, we are so brazen to assume we can, nay WILL, pioneer the future of digital storytelling. We scoff at the idea of ebooks being the end all of digital publishing. We chafe at the restraints put on writer and reader alike by the multi-year process of print media.

Let's work together to restore the intimate bonds and direct collaboration between storyteller and audience. Let's use the technology at our fingertips to do so. Download Fictionite from your app store of choice and become an integral part in discovering the new balance in written storytelling—a balance forged by reader and writer together.

CPSIA information can be obtained
at www.ICGtesting.com
Printed in the USA
FFOW03n0337011117
41734FF